MARY-KATE AND ASHLEY
in ACTION!

Fubble Bubble Trouble

A novelization by Megan Stine
based on the teleplay
by Dianne Dixon

A PARACHUTE PRESS BOOK

Parachute Publishing, L.L.C.
156 Fifth Avenue, Suite 302
New York, NY 10010

Published by
HarperEntertainment
An Imprint of HarperCollins*Publishers*
10 East 53rd Street, New York, NY 10022

Mary-Kate and Ashley in ACTION! books are created and produced by Parachute Press, L.L.C., in cooperation with Dualstar Publications, LLC, an affiliate of Dualstar Entertainment Group, LLC, published by HarperEntertainment, an imprint of HarperCollins Publishers.

ISBN 0-06-009304-8

HarperCollins®, ☙®, and HarperEntertainment™ are trademarks of HarperCollins Publishers Inc.

First printing: December 2002

Printed in China

Visit the on-line book boutique on the World Wide Web at
www.mary-kateandashley.com.

Visit HarperEntertainment on the World Wide Web at
www.harpercollins.com

10 9 8 7 6 5 4 3 2 1

Party Time!

"Hey, everyone! Come and watch!" Ashley called to her friends. "Ivan's going to be on TV in two minutes!"

Ashley and her sister Mary-Kate were at a party. It was for their good friend Ivan Quintero, IQ for short.

Even though Ivan was only fifteen, he was supersmart. He invented all kinds of cool gadgets. Mary-Kate and Ashley used them all the time. Especially when they were on a secret mission.

Most of their friends didn't know it, but Mary-Kate and Ashley were special agents! They worked for a supersecret agency called Headquarters.

"Hey, guys! This is a great party," Rodney Choy told Ashley. He ran his hand through his jet-black hair.

"Thanks!" Ashley said.

Seventeen-year-old Rod worked for Headquarters, too. When Mary-Kate and Ashley were on a mission, Rod drove them wherever they needed to go.

"Hello? May I come in?" a gray-haired woman called from the door. It was Ivan's grandmother! Mary-Kate and Ashley ran to greet her.

"Is this the party for my favorite grandson?" she asked.

"Yes, Mrs. Quintero!" Ashley said. "I'm so glad you came!"

"We thought you might not make it," Mary-Kate said. "It's raining so hard outside."

"Oh, don't worry." Mrs. Quintero smiled. "A little water won't melt me. I'm not made of sugar."

"Are you sure?" Mary-Kate teased. "Because you *are* awfully sweet!"

Mrs. Quintero laughed. Ashley led her into the living room to watch TV with the rest of the guests.

All of Mary-Kate and Ashley's friends gathered around. Soon, everyone would see Ivan on television! He had been named Most Inventive Young Mind of the Decade.

IQ kissed his grandmother hello. Then he sat on the floor, waiting to see himself on TV. "This is so exciting!" he said, adjusting his glasses.

Rod sat close to the set, munching on a new candy called Fubble Bubble. It was a cross between a chocolate bar, cotton candy, and candy corn.

"Slow down, Rod. Save some Fubble Bubble for the rest of us," Ashley teased.

"No way," Rod joked. "This stuff is the best!"

"Look everyone! Here comes my part!" IQ pointed at the TV.

"And now," the TV announcer said, "the Most Inventive Young Mind of the Decade award goes to . . ."

Zzz-zzzz! The TV crackled. The picture turned fuzzy. No one could see a thing!

"Hey! What happened?" Rod asked.

"Fix it—quick!" someone in the crowd yelled.

IQ checked out the set. "There's nothing wrong with this TV. It should be working fine," he reported.

"That's weird," Ashley's friend Kaylie said. "My TV did the same thing yesterday."

"Mine, too!" Mary-Kate's friend Tasha chimed in. "The picture gets fuzzy and wavy all the time. Lots of my friends have the same problem."

Ashley glanced at Mary-Kate.

TVs everywhere were on the fritz? That sounded like trouble!

"We better check this out," Mary-Kate said.

Ashley nodded. "Hey, guys," she whispered to Rod and IQ, "The party can go on without us, but we need to leave."

Mary-Kate picked up her beige Scottie, Quincy. Then Rod, IQ, Quincy, Mary-Kate, and Ashley piled into Rod's car.

"To the jet," Ashley said. "I have a feeling we have a new mission on our hands!"

CHAPTER TWO
Too Much Static

The car squealed away from the curb.

"What's wrong now?" Quincy asked. "Where are we going? What about the party? I was having fun!"

Most people were surprised to find out that Quincy could talk.

They were even more surprised when they discovered that Quincy wasn't a real dog. He was a high-tech special-agent assisting machine! IQ had invented him to help Mary-Kate and Ashley on all their secret missions.

Mary-Kate spoke into her bracelet. "Digital diary—Saturday, one thirty-three P.M. Strange disturbance on TVs noticed around the area. Heading to the jet to check things out."

Ashley smiled. Her sister was always doing that—making notes in her special-agent bracelet computer. Sometimes Ashley wondered if Mary-Kate had become a special agent just for the cool gadgets.

When they reached their private jet, Ashley ran straight to the plane's living room.

"Let's see if this TV is working," Ashley suggested.

"Good idea," Mary-Kate agreed.

Ashley flipped on the television. A dog food commercial blinked onto the screen.

"Look!" Ashley pointed at the TV screen. "This TV is working just fine!"

"That's so weird," Mary-Kate said. "I wonder what's going on?"

Ashley frowned, trying to figure it out.

Rod walked in from the jet's kitchen, munching from another box of Fubble Bubble. "Have you guys come up with any clues yet?" he asked.

"No," Ashley said. She glanced back at the TV.

Wait a minute—now the picture was all fuzzy!

"I mean—yes!" she said. "We *do* have a clue!"

"Really? What?" Rod asked.

Ashley grabbed the box of Fubble Bubble from Rod's hands. She waved the box in front of the TV.

Zzzz-zzzz! The static on the TV grew stronger whenever Rod's box of Fubble Bubble came close to it!

Mary-Kate gasped. "It's the candy!"

"I don't get it," Rod said. "What does the candy have to do with anything?"

"You were eating Fubble Bubble at our party," Ashley explained. "That's when the TV picture went bad."

"And just now you walked in with another box," Mary-Kate went on. "And bang! The picture got fuzzy again."

Ashley and Mary-Kate ran to their computer. They had to find out where Fubble Bubble was made!

Mary-Kate did a quick Internet search. Her eyes lit up. "Guess where the main store and factory is."

"Where?" Ashley asked.

"In the Mall of Malls," Mary-Kate cheered, "the largest indoor shopping center in the world!"

"So, first we solve the case," Ashley said. "Then we take a major shopping break!"

"Okay," IQ said. "But if you go right now, I won't have time to invent any new techno toys for you guys."

"Bummer," Mary-Kate said. "The toys are the best part of the job!"

"Will you be all right without them?" Rod asked.

"Don't worry," Ashley said. "We won't need special-agent gear. We've got our brains! And besides, we're going undercover as factory workers—in a *mall*!"

"Right," Mary-Kate agreed with a nod. "How dangerous can that be?"

CHAPTER THREE

Can't Stop to Shop

Ashley and Mary-Kate hurried through the Mall of Malls. Each of them wore a brand-new Fubble Bubble uniform—pink jackets, white pants, and little white hats.

As they made their way to the Fubble Bubble factory, they gazed around the huge shopping space.

"This place is amazing!" Mary-Kate said. "We've already passed five shoe stores, three music stores, and an awesome hair salon. And we're still near the entrance!"

"*Six* shoe stores," Ashley corrected her sister. "But who's counting?"

Mary-Kate clicked on her special-agent bracelet and began to speak. "We are entering the Fubble Bubble store," she whispered. "Four twenty-nine P.M."

Ashley flipped on her spy bracelet, too. In it, she stored facts and information about the places she visited.

"Did you know that Fubble Bubble sells eighteen million dollars' worth of candy every month?" Ashley asked her sister. "They have sixty-three stores in forty different cities. And . . ."

"Never mind the facts," Mary-Kate said. "Here comes our new boss!"

Ashley glanced up from her bracelet. A bulky red-haired boy with an angry look on his face marched toward her. His name tag said MARCO.

"Get out of here!" he screamed at them. "I mean it! Get out of here right now!"

CHAPTER FOUR
Bad News Boss

Yikes! Ashley jumped back.

"What's his problem?" she whispered to Mary-Kate.

"I don't know," Mary-Kate said. "But he certainly doesn't seem like a nice guy."

"Maybe he has something to do with the TV trouble," Ashley guessed. "Let's keep an eye on him!"

Marco bent down and scowled at something behind the girls. Ashley whirled around. It was Quincy! He had been tagging along behind them.

"No dogs allowed," Marco said. "It's against the rules in a candy store. Get out—now!"

Quincy scampered away.

Ashley watched as he hid around the

corner near the entrance to the store. She smiled. Quincy was always there when she needed him. He really was a special agent's best friend!

"Marco, what are you doing?" someone asked. Ashley turned to see an older teenage girl coming out of the back room. Her reddish brown hair was pulled into a big poufy ponytail. She wore a cute short purple-and-pink dress.

"You know it's *my* job to welcome the new employees," the girl told Marco. She turned to Ashley "Hi! I'm Suzi."

Ashley smiled. "I'm Amber," she said, using her special-agent name.

"And I'm Misty." Mary-Kate gave her own special-agent name. "We're your new trainees!"

"Welcome to Fubble Bubble!" Suzi said in a supercheery voice. "Wow! You two really remind me of each other. Are you best friends or something?"

Is she kidding? Ashley wondered. Can't she see that we're related?

"We're sisters," Mary-Kate said.

"Really?" Suzi asked, surprised. "That's cool!" She gave them a big smile. "Follow me and we'll get you started."

Ashley rolled her eyes and whispered to Mary-Kate. "She's nice, but she's not very smart."

"I know," Mary-Kate joked quietly. "We should keep her out of the way while we check out what's really going on around here."

Suzi led Mary-Kate and Ashley through the Fubble Bubble factory. She explained each step of how Fubble Bubble was made.

"Excuse me," Mary-Kate said. "But what happens to the candy in there?" She pointed to a conveyor belt carrying tons of Fubble Bubble candy. The candy rode the belt into a closed-off room.

"Oh, that?" Suzi said. "That's where they put in the secret ingredient."

"Really? What *is* the secret ingredient?" Ashley asked.

Suzi giggled. "It's what makes the candy taste so good!"

Ashley glanced at Mary-Kate. That wasn't very helpful information.

Suzi led the sisters to their work stations. "Marco will tell you what to do," she said. "He's your boss."

"Really?" Mary-Kate asked. "Does he have to be our—"

"Quiet!" Marco shouted. "You're already behind schedule."

"Have fun!" Suzi called. She walked away.

Quickly, Marco showed Mary-Kate and

Ashley how to use the machines to make Fubble Bubble candy.

Ashley liked her job. When the candy came along the conveyor belt, she got to squirt a giant bag of chocolate frosting on each piece.

Mary-Kate had to spray baking sheets with oil. Then she pulled a cord overhead, and globs of raw candy dropped down onto the sheets.

Ashley squirted the chocolate carefully.

Marco watched her every moment. When he finally took a break, Ashley leaned closer to her sister.

"Someone should follow Marco," she whispered. "He is so mean, he has to be the one interfering with TVs all over America."

"I think so, too," Mary-Kate said. "But we need some backup if we're going to find out for sure."

Mary-Kate flipped open her bracelet. She pressed a button to call Quincy, using a secret radar signal.

A moment later Quincy leaped up onto the conveyor belt. "Hi!" he said. "What's up?"

The conveyor belt kept moving. Quincy had to walk in the opposite direction to stay in one place!

"We need someone to tail Marco," Ashley explained.

"And since you're the one with the tail," Mary-Kate joked, "we thought you could do it!"

"I'm on it!" Quincy trotted off.

Ashley continued to squirt chocolate. Then she felt a tickle in her nose.

"Uh-oh. I think I'm going to . . . going to . . . aaah-*chooo*!" Ashley squeezed her frosting bag with one hand. Chocolate frosting squirted everywhere!

Her other hand flew up—and knocked into Mary-Kate.

"Yikes!" Mary-Kate lost her balance. She hung on to her cord to steady herself.

"Look out!" Ashley cried. A tremendous pile of candy globs fell from the ceiling.

"Aaahhh!" Mary-Kate yelled. "What should we do?"

"Quick—grease the cookie sheets!" Ashley called. "Get as many as you can into the oven!"

Mary-Kate aimed the spray gun. She pressed the trigger as hard as she could.

Whoooosh! Oil squirted everywhere.

Clang! Clang! Cookie sheets fell off the slick conveyor belt.

Quincy ran back into the factory. "Girls, you're never going to believe what I found—whoooooooa!" He stepped on a cookie sheet and slid across the floor.

Crash! He slammed into a wall.

Ashley glanced around. What a mess! Half a day of work and already everything was covered in goo!

"This day can't get any worse," Mary-Kate said.

Ashley gasped. "Yes, it can!"

Marco walked in the door.

Oh, no! Ashley thought. He's going to fire us! And then we'll never find out about his secret plan!

Marco stared at the cookie sheets lying on the floor—and at the goo covering Mary-Kate and Ashley. "What happened here?" he asked.

"We can explain!" Mary-Kate said.

"Well, not exactly *explain*," Ashley admitted. "But we can make up a really good story!"

"That's okay." Marco shrugged. "Don't worry about the mess. I can clean it up."

Ashley's eyes popped open wide. "You can?"

"Yes," Marco said. "But I want to talk to you first."

"What about?" Mary-Kate asked.

"I'm tired of hiding all the time," Marco said. "I have to confess."

"I knew it!" Ashley whispered to Mary-Kate. "He's the bad guy! We were so right!"

"What do you want to confess about?" Mary-Kate asked Marco.

"Please don't think I'm bad," Marco said. "But I have to tell the truth. I'm totally crazy about Fubble Bubble."

Huh? Ashley frowned. *That* was Marco's confession?

"Whenever nobody's watching," Marco continued, "I stuff my pockets with candy."

"So you're a thief?" Mary-Kate asked.

"Not really," Marco said. "I take only the little broken pieces that would be thrown out anyway. But I go outside to eat them—when I *should* be working. Your dog caught me doing just that."

Marco gave Quincy a pat on the head.
"I feel so bad about it. That's why I was
mean to you before. I'm sorry."

Ashley nodded. She could see that
Marco was telling the truth.

"I don't want to get in trouble with the
owner of this place," Marco went on. "So
I'm trying to stop sneaking candy bits.
Will you help me?"

Quincy jumped into Marco's arms and
licked his face.

"Sure," Mary-Kate said.

"Definitely," Ashley agreed.

"Thanks. You guys are the best," Marco said.

Then he started to clean up the mess.

"We were so wrong about him!" Ashley whispered.

"So wrong," Mary-Kate said. "Just because he wasn't fun and happy all the time, we thought that he was the bad guy."

The girls bent down to help Marco clean up.

While Ashley worked, she thought about their mission. They *still* had to find out how Fubble Bubble was messing with TVs all over the country.

"Marco, what can you tell me about the owner of this place?" Ashley asked.

"Miss Bates?" Marco said. He shivered. "She scares me. She's very smart, very tough, and really cold."

"Bates?" Ashley glanced at her sister. "Do you mean Romy Bates?"

"Yes!" Marco answered. "You know about her?"

"Oh, yeah," Mary-Kate said. "We know lots about her."

"And it's all bad!" Ashley added. "Romy Bates is the most evil young genius in the world! Wherever Romy goes, trouble is sure to follow."

Mary-Kate turned to her. "If Romy owns this place, we had better take a good look around—late at night, while no one is watching."

"Good idea," Ashley agreed. "Marco, can you use your key to let us in here tonight? After closing, when everyone has gone home?"

"I guess so," Marco said. "But what if Miss Bates finds out? It could be very dangerous."

"We know," Ashley agreed. "But we don't have any choice. Romy Bates is evil."

"And if we know anything about her, she is probably using Fubble Bubble as part of a plan to take over the planet!" Mary-Kate finished.

"Which means," Ashley went on, "that we've got to save the world . . . again!"

That night the Fubble Bubble factory was dark and quiet. Ashley and Mary-Kate sneaked inside. Ashley carried Quincy in her backpack.

"Where to?" Mary-Kate asked.

"To the secret ingredient room," Ashley answered. "Let's find out what the big *secret* is!"

Together Mary-Kate and Ashley crawled along the conveyor belt. The belt led them into a tube as they moved closer to the secret room.

Ashley shined her flashlight ahead.

"We sure did mess up about Marco," Ashley said as she crawled. "I can't believe how wrong we were. Just because he was shy and grumpy, we thought he was a criminal."

"I know," Mary-Kate agreed. "I guess that old saying is true. You can't judge a book by its cover."

"Right," Ashley said. "Like the biggest airhead in the world could be . . ."

"Not so dumb after all!" Mary-Kate finished her sentence.

"Wait a minute," Ashley said. "The biggest airhead in the world? That sounds like Suzi! Maybe she isn't as dumb—or as nice—as she looks!"

"Do you think Suzi is working with Romy Bates?" Mary-Kate asked.

Before Ashley could answer, a voice blared over the factory's speaker system.

"Good-bye, special agents! Sweet dreams!"

"Suzi!" Ashley recognized the voice
right away.

"Whoa!" Mary-Kate cried. The conveyor
belt started moving. It carried them up a
ramp.

Then Ashley heard a rumbling noise.
"What's that?" she asked.

Mary-Kate's mouth hung open. She pointed down the tube—at a huge wave of hot chocolate goo! It was flowing straight toward them.

"Mary-Kate!" Ashley cried. "Run!"

CHAPTER SIX
Chocolate-Covered Trouble

Mary-Kate and Ashley ran down the tube. Ahead of them, the conveyor belt ended. Ashley peeked over the edge. It was a long way down!

"Oh, no! We're trapped!" Ashley cried. Behind them, the huge wave of chocolate closed in.

"Jump!" Mary-Kate ordered.

"Aaaahhh!" Ashley screamed as she and Mary-Kate leaped off the end of the conveyor belt.

They were falling . . . falling . . .

"Ooof!" Ashley landed in a huge vat of chocolate. Actually, it just looked like chocolate. It was really filled with chocolate candy chips!

"Are you okay?" Mary-Kate asked.

"I'm fine," Ashley answered. "But where did Quincy go?"

Mary-Kate dug around in the chips, looking for Quincy. Finally she pulled him out and brushed the sticky candy out of his fur.

"Quincy! I'm so glad you're okay!" Mary-Kate gave her dog a hug.

Quincy shook his head. "So am I!" he replied.

Ashley gazed up at the ceiling. Two huge electric beaters hung down, ready to dip into the vat. Each beater looked big enough to crush a car!

"Let's get out of here," Ashley said. "Before Suzi decides to turn this thing on."

Whrrrrr. The beater motor started to hum.

"Too late!" Mary-Kate cried.

Ashley leaped for the edge of the vat. She pulled hard to hoist herself up. Mary-Kate and Quincy scrambled up onto the other side of the vat.

Just in time! The giant metal beaters dropped down and began to stir the candy chips. Then a flood of hot, sticky goo poured into the vat.

"Wow," Ashley said. "We could have been smashed! Suzi is just as evil as Romy Bates!"

"We've been wrong about a *lot* of people lately," Mary-Kate admitted.

"Still, we were right about one thing," Ashley said. "This is the secret room—and these chips must be the secret weapon Romy is using to ruin the TVs."

"How could they be?" Quincy asked. "They're just sugar."

"That's not all they are," Mary-Kate said. She held up a few chips to the light. "Look!"

Ashley noticed strange lines running through the chips. The pattern reminded her of something. . . .

"Computer chips!" Ashley gasped. "Of course! Romy Bates is a computer genius. These candy computer chips must be programmed to mess up TV signals whenever they're close to a TV set."

"But . . . why?" Mary-Kate wondered.

Ashley heard footsteps above them. She glanced up.

There, on a metal walkway high above their heads, stood Suzi—and Romy Bates.

Romy smiled. "My next truckload of Fubble Bubble is about to go out to countries all over the globe," she said. "Then I'll be able to control all the TVs everywhere! People will be able to watch only what I want them to—me! Romy TV twenty-four hours a day, seven days a week! And then I will rule the world."

"Romy, that's so wrong," Mary-Kate said sadly. "You need serious help."

"I don't think so," Romy said. "This will teach people who is the most inventive mind of the decade. Me!"

Romy smiled. "And now I'm ready to watch my shipment of chips as it leaves. Bye-bye, special agents! I hope you're comfy down there."

Romy and Suzi walked out of the vat room. The doors slammed shut behind them.

"I can't believe this," Mary-Kate wailed. "We're trapped down here!"

"And Romy is getting away!" Ashley said. "What do we do now?"

CHAPTER SEVEN
No Way Out

"We can't give up," Ashley said. "I refuse to be beaten by that snotty, smirking Romy Bates with her stupid, sneaky—"

"Wait! Stop!" Mary-Kate cried.

"What?" Ashley wondered. "Too many *s* words?"

"No," Mary-Kate said. *"Beaten!"* Mary-Kate pointed up at the ceiling. "Those beaters are our ticket out of here!"

Ashley blinked. Really? She didn't quite see how. The beaters were too high and out of reach.

Mary-Kate explained her plan. "The beaters started moving when we fell into the vat. Maybe our weight triggered the beaters to come down."

"I get it!" Ashley cried. "So if we jump down into the vat, maybe the beaters will drop down again!"

"And then we can hitch a ride out of here!"

"Let's go for it!" Quincy said.

On the count of three, the girls jumped into the container. They landed on their feet with a loud bang!

Whrrrrr. The giant beaters turned on and began to lower.

"It worked! Flatten yourself against the wall!" Mary-Kate shouted.

The huge metal paddles whizzed and whirred in a crazy pattern. Ashley hurried to get out of the way. Her knees shook as she pressed her back up against the wall of the vat. If one of the beaters hit her, it would squash her flat!

Mary-Kate held Quincy tightly to her chest.

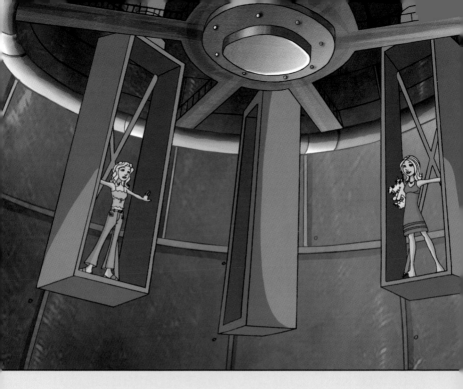

Finally the beaters stopped whirring.

"Now's our chance!" Ashley called out. "Grab on!"

She and Mary-Kate climbed onto the beaters.

Slowly, the beaters began to lift up again.

"We did it!" Mary-Kate called. The three of them rode the beaters up, up, toward the ceiling. Then they stepped off the beaters onto the metal walkway.

They raced out of the front of the building—and found Marco waiting outside.

"What now?" he asked.

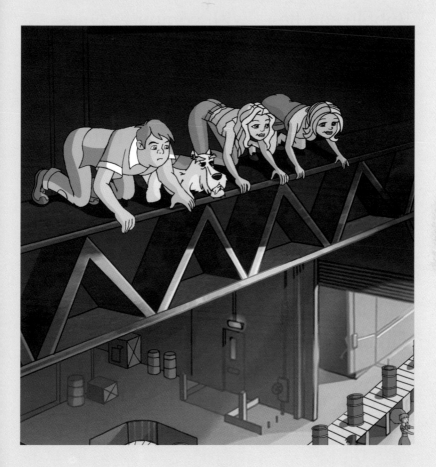

"Now we have to stop Romy—somehow!" Ashley said.

They sneaked around to the loading dock. Romy Bates and Suzi watched as Fubble Bubble workers loaded up their trucks. Huge barrels full of Fubble Bubble candies—with computer chips inside—were piled up everywhere.

Rain poured down, soaking the parking lot.

"What should we do?" Mary-Kate wondered.

"I don't know!" Ashley admitted. "We don't have any new special-agent gadgets to help us out now."

"Yeah," Mary-Kate agreed. "I wish we had some great big techno toy that would zap all those computer chips in a flash!"

Ashley stepped in a puddle.

"Wait a minute!" she cried. "We *do* have something! Something better than

techno toys! We've got the rain!"

Mary-Kate's eyes lit up. "You mean . . . ?"

"Remember what IQ's grandmother said? She said a little rain wouldn't melt her because she wasn't made of sugar!" Ashley cried.

"But those candy chips *are* made of sugar!" Mary-Kate blurted out.

"And the rain is coming down in buckets!" Marco cheered.

Ashley scanned the loading dock. A conveyor belt was moving all the barrels of chips toward the open truck.

"Follow my lead," Ashley said. "I have a plan."

Both girls leaped up onto the loading dock. "Well, Romy, it looks like your little plan is all wet," Ashley said.

"You!" Romy cried. "How did you . . ." She shook her head. "It doesn't matter. You're too late. My truck will be loaded up and ready to go in just a minute. But first I'll be happy to take care of you."

She and Suzi jumped into action. They were ready to fight. But Ashley and Mary-Kate were faster.

Ashley grabbed a carton of Fubble Bubble. She threw it at Suzi and knocked her down.

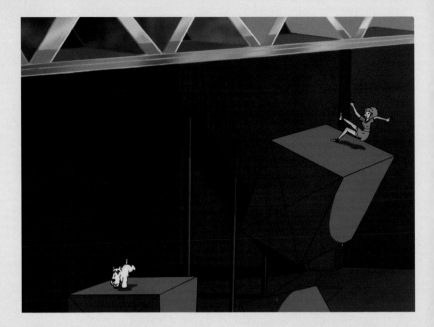

Mary-Kate rolled a big barrel toward Romy. Romy had to leap aside to avoid being hit.

"Nice try," Romy said. "But you special agents aren't worth any more trouble. And my truck is ready to go. I'm out of here!"

Without looking, she jumped off the loading dock toward her open truck.

But the truck was gone! Marco had

released the brake. The truck had rolled downhill!

Romy landed on the ground. So did all her barrels of Fubble Bubble chips! When they fell, the barrels broke open. The pouring rain melted all of the candy inside, leaving nothing but a big pile of sticky goo.

"Nooooooo!" Romy screamed when she saw the big mess she'd landed in. "My chips! My plan! My genius!"

Ashley and Mary-Kate gave each other high fives.

Mary-Kate opened her special-agent bracelet. She hit the phone button. "IQ? It's Mary-Kate. Call Headquarters and let them know another one of Romy Bates's evil plans is all wet!"

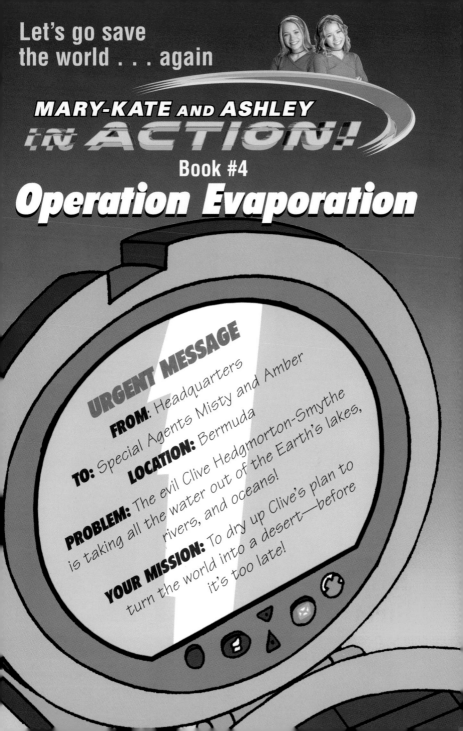

mary-kateandashley

awholenewlook

the animated tv series...now in a book series

It's
What
YOU
Read.

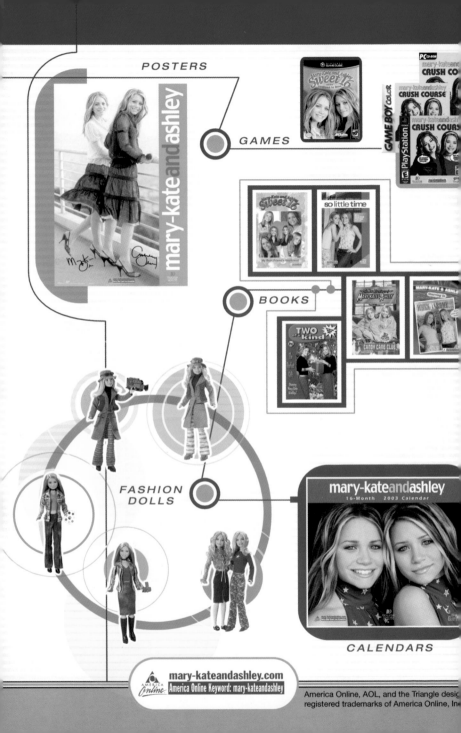

POSTERS

GAMES

BOOKS

FASHION DOLLS

mary-kateandashley
16-Month 2003 Calendar

CALENDARS